THIS BOOK BELONGS TO

Icon Publishing Limited
P. O. Box OD 972
Odorkor, Accra
Ghana
www.facebook.com/myicongh
www.twitter.com/myicongh
+233 (0)23 3505 055,

iconpublishingltd@gmail.com
iconpublishing@ymail.com
enquiries.icongh@gmail.com

Cover and Interior Design by iCON-gh +233 24 4890 432

ISBN: 978-9988-8566-7-0

AFRICAN FOLKTALE SERIES

THE EVIL KING WHO DESTROYED HIMSELF

A NIGERIAN FOLKTALE

Dan Odei

Kwame Insaidoo

An Ibo folktale from Nigeria that depicts the evil shenanigans of a tyrant king and his eventual downfall.

Long, long ago, a wicked and dictatorial king was installed in a big town. He was feared for his wickedness, savagery, and barbarity in the town and all the neighbouring lands. One cloudy and rainy day, he issued a decree that required any woman who gave birth to a baby boy to send the baby to the king's palace at once for a kingly blessing. Anyone who disobeyed the king's decree would immediately be put to death by hanging in the public square.

Not a single woman in the kingdom dared disobey the king's decree because of the king's wickedness, brutal, and inhumane abuse of women who failed to comply with his orders. Any woman who gave birth to a boy sent him to the king's palace. After the boy was received in the palace, the king's executioners would ask the woman to leave at once so they could perform their rituals on the child, but the plain truth was that once the mother left the baby boy was hacked to death.

This barbaric and odious decree of killing boys and keeping only baby girls became the law of the land and went on for many, many years. The women of the town got to know the fate of the baby boys they sent to the palace because it was an open secret that the baby boys were killed by the king's executioners. But, because of their fear of the savage king, no one dared challenge him, and instead they slavishly obeyed him and continued to take all their newborn baby boys to his palace.

One day a beautiful woman gave birth to a handsome baby boy and decided to defy the king's decree by refusing to send her baby to the palace. Instead she hid the baby so she could look at him every day. The woman concealed the baby in a basket and put it in a river. She fed the baby for a month, but the king's ubiquitous executioners became suspicious of her activities. She resolved that the savage king would not get the chance to execute her baby and declared, "This beastly king will never get the chance to touch my handsome baby boy."

She wrote a short, crisp note that read thus: "We live in a horrible land, where our savage and barbaric king has decreed that all baby boys be put to death, but I swore that I would not kill my little prince. So if you come across this baby, please love him with all your heart and take great care of him, because one day he will be a great man." She put the note in the baby's basket, covered it, and pushed it to the centre of a larger river where the currents were strong.

The basket floated on the river for many days until it reached a new town where such odious killings did not exist. As fate would have it, an old lady in the new town saw a basket floating in the river and called on a couple of strong men to swim out and fetch the basket for her. When they returned with the basket, the old lady opened it and beheld the handsome baby boy wrapped in immaculate white linen with a note begging for whoever opened the basket to take good care of the boy. Upon reading the note, the woman took the baby home and took great care of him.

Gradually, the baby grew up and became a man, a really handsome man as his mother had said when he was an infant, and was loved by all the people of the town. He was very industrious and helped the townsfolk to build many houses, and he was able to farm hundreds of acres of corn and other crops.

*The beautiful woman gently pushing the baby's basket to the
centre of the large river.*

His hard work endeared him to his fellow townsfolk whose admiration of him and his upright manner led them to collectively elect him as their king. He became a popular and benevolent ruler who decreed that no person in his town was to be killed or harmed by executioners or members of the royal family. He adored and protected his people, and the people, for their part, loved and adored him back. He ensured that the laws of the land were fair and just and that they did not unnecessarily intimidate any citizen.

One day the king made a trip to the town where he had been born, in search of his real mother; but the savage and tyrannical king was still in power. His decree regarding male children had not been repealed, so baby boys were still dying just as soon as they were born.

His mother was thrilled to finally see her son, but, fortunately or unfortunately for him, the tyrant king's beautiful daughter also saw him—this attractive and handsome benevolent king from another town—and threw herself at his feet and asked for his hand in marriage. The benevolent king refused and instead said to his servants, "Remove this daughter of the tyrant king from my mother's house and from my sight at once." His orders were obeyed, and the tyrant's king's daughter was thrown out of the house.

The king's daughter was hurt by the outright rejection of her marriage offer and felt disgraced by the manner in which she had been thrown out of a commoner's house. She vowed to avenge the sad spectacle and abuse she had endured in the house.

She complained to her father, the tyrant king, about the horrible and disgraceful treatment she had endured at the hands of the so-called benevolent king from the nearby town. Her father assured her not to worry at all because he knew how to fix him and destroy all his kingship nonsense. He would ensure that through any means, foul or fair, this so-called king would end up in one of his many dungeons fit only for criminals.

The tyrant king set out to destroy the benevolent king by asking his wise counsellors to trace his ancestral roots to find out who the benevolent king's parents were, where he had been born, what sort of person he had been before he grew up, and what skeletons were hidden in his closet—and then reveal all this to his people.

The counsellors diligently accomplished their dirt digging and found out that the benevolent king had been born in their very own town. They hurriedly reported this to their king: "The so-called benevolent king is one of us! He was born in our town but was shipped to the neighbouring town by his mother."

The tyrant king sent message to his elders, counsellors, executioners, king makers, and all the queens of the nearby town informing them that their so-called benevolent king was not originally from their town at all, but had been born in his town. The message continued, "Both of his parents are still alive today in my town. You know that because he is a foreigner, he cannot be a king in your town, as the traditional laws and customs of your town dictate. Woe betide your town if you refuse to depose him. The unrest and insurrection that will befall your town will consume all your people in unquenchable flames, and I know you don't want that, because you are peace-loving people."

Even though the people of the town loved their king with all their hearts, their hands were tied by this revelation. So after a tedious investigation and elaborate double-checking of their information, it was revealed that their king was in fact a foreigner who had migrated from the neighbouring town and could not by their customary and traditional laws be the king of their town. The next day he was promptly deposed from the throne.

The man set sail back to the town where his mother and father still resided and came to live happily with his parents—but this happiness did not last long, because of the king's daughter.

One day, as the man was home talking with his mother, the king's daughter arrived, accompanied by the King's executioners, and they arrested him for being rude, insolent, disrespectful, and hostile to her when she had proposed to marry him. They put him in one of the king's dungeons, and in the middle of the night when everybody was asleep, the daughter entered the jailhouse and whispered in the man's ear, "Please kiss me. Make love to me right here, and I will ensure that the guards set you free tomorrow so we can leave this town and live happily ever after." The man, faced with this tempting proposal from the king's beautiful daughter, looked to the ceiling of the jail and began to sing:

The king's daughter is asking for trouble to befall her
The king's daughter is really courting trouble
The king's daughter should know she is in for a rude awakening
Because your father the wicked king made an evil decree
That all baby boys born in his town be executed
Today, unbeknownst to you, I was the boy hidden in the river
That the king's daughter has fallen madly in love with
And the king's daughter is my worst enemy
Whose actions led me to lose my kingship
And so the king's daughter is indeed my worst enemy

The king's daughter was surprised at the man's discipline—that, as beautiful as she was and with all her seductive advances, he had refused her and even pushed her away from him. She could not believe that any man had that level of self-control and discipline to resist her beauty and charms. Yet she persisted, throwing herself on him and forcing a kiss, which he promptly refused. As much as the king's daughter tried to seduce the man, he stubbornly refused all her advances and looked up to the ceiling and began singing his song again.

The daughter retreated and went back to her palace to plan yet another attack to seduce this man whom she was madly in love with. She vowed to do anything under the sun to win his love. When she returned to the jail, she took off all her clothes and stood naked in the room before this poor man. She was bent upon torturing him until he gave in to her sexual fantasies and voluntarily surrender to her wishes. Once again the man looked up to the ceiling and burst out into his song again.

When the man finished singing his song, the king's daughter went closer to him and said, "I do not care how many times you sing that crazy song of yours ... I am madly in love with you, and since I am the daughter of the great king, you are mine."

She paused to hear what he had to say, but the man did not utter a word. So she continued, "If you do not make love to me and you keep disgracing me like this, I will call the guards and tell them that you have forced yourself on me, attacked me, and attempted to rape me. You see, they will believe me because I am naked here in the jail in the middle of the night."

The man looked into her eyes and became even more disgusted with her lies and her vulgar and perverted morality and what she was attempting to do to him. She continued to threaten him, saying, "My father will kill you if I go and tell him that I was visiting all the prisoners in the jailhouse and you came and raped me. If you do not want my father to torture you, you better lie down with me now, and I will save you from this miserable place." She went down on her knees to beg him to lie down with her, but once again the man looked up to the ceiling and burst out singing:

The king's daughter is asking for trouble to befall her
The king's daughter is really courting trouble
The king's daughter should know she is in for a rude awakening
Because your father, the wicked king made an evil decree
That all baby boys born in his town be executed
Today, unbeknownst to you, I was the boy hidden in the river
That the king's daughter has fallen madly in love with
And the king's daughter is my worst enemy
Whose actions led me to lose my kingship
And so the king's daughter is indeed my worst enemy

The man sang and sang, repeating the same song over and over again. The daughter became so annoyed that she screamed for help from her father's guards. She threw herself onto the ground and began to sob uncontrollably, accusing the man of attacking her and attempting to rape her. The guards rushed in, flung the doors wide open, and found the princess naked and the prisoner looking up the ceiling singing his song. The guards carried the man away to the king's palace and informed him of the apparent attack on his daughter by the singing prisoner.

The daughter told her father, "Father, this man is the most abusive prisoner you have ever had in your jails. When I went into the jails to help feed the prisoners, he attacked me and attempted to rape me, so I screamed and yelled for the guards to save me from this mad rapist."

The king asked the head guard to describe what he had seen when he arrived at the jail cell after hearing the daughter scream for help. The guard answered, "Mighty king, around midnight we heard a loud scream and a shrill voice inside the jailhouse, so we rushed in to see your daughter, naked, lying on the floor, and weeping bitterly."

The king asked his daughter to explain to him what business she had in the jailhouse in the middle of the night and why she had entered the cell of this particular man who had previously refused to marry her.

The daughter replied, "As an act of mercy and to show the world that you are a benevolent king and not a tyrant, I occasionally make my rounds in the middle of the night to ensure that the prisoners are well cared for and given the right amount of food. Today when I entered into this savage beast's room, he violently tore all my clothes and tried to rape me."

The king asked the prisoner to defend himself against all the charges levelled by the king's daughter. The king added, "These charges could be false, but I need for you to explain to me why I should not kill you for attempting to rape my daughter tonight." The prisoner looked up to the ceiling and began to sing his usual song.

The king roared in extreme anger, "How dare you challenge our laws, you saucy fool? You common slave! You naughty fool! You attempt to rape my daughter and disobey our laws, and when I ask you to explain yourself to me, what I get from you is a stupid, mumbo jumbo song. You shall be killed, and your carcass spread in front of my pets, so that our people will learn from your insolence."

The prisoner is standing before the king with hands tied

Just as the king was about to order his executioners to hang the man, his daughter interceded and told her father, "Father, do not waste your time and dignity to spill his worthless blood on our land. It will be better to banish him from our land. This banishment will hurt him the most because he will never set his eyes again on his parents or his loved ones in our land. Just killing him is inappropriate because he stands to lose nothing."

The king agreed with his daughter and put the man in an open canoe with a small provision of food and asked him to leave in the middle of the night. The daughter felt sorry for him and asked her father to give him a ship, which the king promptly refused to do. Once again the man was to sail down the very river that his mother had been forced to place him in as a baby in a basket. Toward midnight the king's daughter went to the canoe and loaded it with all sorts of food and drinks and even expensive clothing that her own father had used on important occasions. After that she went to the jailhouse where the man was, apologized to him for all the bad things she had done to him, and kissed the floor where he slept—since the man refused to kiss her—and bade him farewell. When the clock struck midnight, the guards opened the jailhouse and escorted the man to his canoe. They pushed the canoe into the water, bade him farewell, and told him never to return again to their land.

The man was left on his own in the middle of the night; but he was lucky to be alive, and he swore that he would do everything in his power to sail safely across the huge river to the other side where he would be accepted as a human being and not as a prisoner.

It took him an entire week to successfully sail across the water, and finally he reached a town he had never been to. He went to their king to beg for land to live on and farm. He promised the king that when he harvested his food, he would help feed some of the poor in the area. The king of the land was so impressed with the man's honesty and generosity that he gave him many acres of fertile land near the river to farm on. The hardworking man planted corn, beans, yams, and plantains, and raised all sorts of goats, sheep, cows, and even had hundreds of chicken. Fortunately for this man, all his farm products and his domestic animals multiplied in large numbers, so much so that he became a wealthy man who fed many of the hungry and poor people in the town.

Meanwhile as the years passed by, the land of the tyrant king, where the man's mother still lived, was experiencing one of the worst famines in their town's history. Almost everybody there was starving to death. The beautiful daughter of the king, the only princess of the land, was starving to death and had grown so lean, bony, pale, and sick-looking that it was impossible to identify her as the beautiful princess of the land. The people in the town had twice revolted against the tyrant king because they asserted that he was corrupt, brutal, unjust, and unlucky, which had brought them the horrible famine in the land. Because the king was afraid of being dethroned by outsiders due to the incessant riots over food, he decreed, "It is expressly forbidden for any of our citizens to leave our town, nor should outsiders be invited in."

In the midst of the famine riots, the wealthy man who had been banished from the town disguised himself and sailed quietly to his native land, unseen by any of the king's officials. He went straight to his mother's house, but the people still rioting recognized him and clamoured to make him their king because of all his pristine qualities, his hardworking nature, and his love for his people. They gave him a sword to go and kill their king and take his place as their new king. The entire town followed him, and he led the way with his sword and entered the king's palace.

When the tyrant king saw the man with his sword, he also drew his sword, and they both began insulting each other, calling each other all sorts of names and getting ready to fight. When the king's daughter saw what was happening, she stood between them in utter amazement.

In her anger, she went to her room, took her sword, and then came back and killed her father, the king, thinking that once he was dead, she would get the chance once more to seduce the man she was still in love with. Unfortunately for her, however, once the king was killed, the man took his sword and killed the king's daughter. Both the king and his daughter were now dead.

All the people of the town were united on one accord to install the man as their next king. The new king spoke at a big gathering attended by all the townsfolk. He told the people, "Today is the new day that you have struggled long and hard to achieve. The bloody days of executing baby boys are over; no baby boy will be killed in this land again. We shall preserve all boys and girls born in our land because they are all sent to us by almighty God to be a blessing to our motherland."

The new king continued, "This horrible famine we are all experiencing today is because we have incurred God's wrath for killing all baby boys for almost half a century. God is angry with us because of our evil ways, which have led us to keep only women in our land and destroy all the boys who could have worked hard with their women to cultivate the land and bring plenty of food to our people."

The king further added, "Today there is virtually no man in this land, but everywhere you look, there are women, women, women, and more women. But we should remind all of you that when God first created the world he made a man and put him above all other things, but because man was not satisfied to be alone, he gave him a woman. And God said the 'woman' means 'woe unto man,' a big curse unto man because man was stubbornly unsatisfied with all the creations God gave him. The calamities, the famine, all the insurrection in the land, and other evils that have befallen this place are the direct consequences of killing all baby boys and keeping all the women. This land is full of women who are a curse to man, and so our land is full of curses, curses, curses, and more curses. They have cursed the land, hence all the problems and calamities in our land."

The new king imported many men from the town where he had all his farms and property to come and marry some of the women in the land. Some greedy men married three; some, two; and others married four wives. And this is what made polygamy an accepted traditional marriage practice in their land.

Moral Lessons

In terms of moral lessons to be drawn from this story, we must first note that the new king had a lot of lessons to learn himself! He quite ignorantly asserted that the presence of abundant women was a curse to the land, resulting in calamities, famine, hazards, evil, and revolt in the land. What he should have preached to his people was that the pernicious actions and decisions of the tyrant king, who had decreed that all baby boys be killed at birth, were what precipitated the revolts, misfortune, and curses in the land, and not the number of women living in the kingdom. Additionally, since the king was a product of a woman, who was supposedly cursed, then the king himself must also be cursed, in which case the curse in the land would have been the result of both the women and men living in the land.

It is also instructive to remind the king that his very existence, his life, and his ascension to the throne were due to a woman; a woman gave birth to him, and the same woman had sense enough to save his life from the cruel tyranny of the king by hiding him in a basket in a river and making his survival and his very existence possible. How could he then have the audacity to utter senseless statements about women being the curse of his land? Furthermore, the tyrant king's daughter actually saved the new king from being executed by his father and ensured that his life was spared. She also killed her own father, which allowed him to become the new king of the land. So, in truth, he owed a lot of gratitude to women who made it possible for him to attain his kingship in the town.

ACTIVITIES

Attempt answering the following questions:

1. Why was the evil king feared?
2. What did the evil king and his executioners do to baby boys who were brought to the palace?
3. What did one woman who had given birth to a handsome baby boy do?
4. a) Who found the baby boy in the basket and how was he rescued?
   b) Why was the handsome baby boy installed as king of the land when he grew up?
5. a) What led to the revelation of the true identity of the benevolent king?
   b) What transpired afterwards?
6. a) During his imprisonment, what did the deposed king do anytime the princess tried to seduce him?
   b) What offense led to his banishment?
   c) What was the first thing he did upon reaching the next village and how did he utilize the opportunity given him?
7. a) Who murdered the evil king?
   b) What became of the daughter after his death?
8. Who was installed as the next king of the big town?

9. What was the cause of the great famine in the land?

10. What have you learned from this folktale?

11. Find the meaning of the following words in the dictionary and use them in sentences of your own,

i. Dictatorial
ii. Barbarity
iii. Savagery
iv. Inhuman
v. Executioners
vi. Hacked
vii. Slavishly
viii. Ubiquitous
ix. Immaculate
x. Endeared
xi. Intimidate
xii. Tyrannical
xiii. Repealed
xiv. Dungeon
xv. Insurrection
xvi. Depose
xvii. Insolent
xviii. Seductive
xix. Retreated
xx. Torturing
xxi. Disgusted
xxii. Vulgar
xxiii. Perverted
xxiv. Flung
xxv. Shrill
xxvi. Carcass
xxvii. Interceded
xxviii. Revolted
xxix. Clamoured

12. In paragraph 1, what does the description of the king 'MAINLY' show?

a. The King was a loving King
b. He was a very powerful King
c. He was an extremely cruel King
d. He was very popular.

25

Answer the questions here.